FIFO

What really happens after the plane takes off...

Aaron Weston

www.facebook.com/aaronwestonauthor

www.instagram.com/aaronwestonauthor

DEDICATION

I dedicate this book to all of the fantastic FIFO workers and their families. I hope that you enjoy the book.

DISCLAIMER

This book is a work of fiction. All characters and events in this book are fictitious and any resemblance to real persons, living or dead is purely coincidental.

ISBN-13: 978-0994391582

Hi, I am Mick, and I work as a dump truck operator on a mine in Western Australia. I do FIFO, which means I fly up to a mine site; work for 1 to 5 weeks, then fly out of that mine site or the closest airport, home for a week or more.

When I first heard about FIFO, I thought, Wow! I am going to be jet setting around Australia, like a rock star.

What it actually means is getting up at a ridiculously early hour, to try to make it to the airport in time. Only to be, surrounded by 20 or more of your half-asleep workmates, who cannot stop whinging about how they have to go to work, and there must be a better way to make money.

This particular morning I was sitting with Deb, who operates the wheel loader. We were drinking our airport purchased coffees and watching the planes taking off. She was banging on about how her daughter, who is 13 now, is going through puberty, and due to all of the changes in her hormone levels, is being a right little bitch and blah, blah, blah, blah. I usually try to pay attention to Deb's stories, but today I could not concentrate, not just, because it was a boring story. I have been through a lot myself lately, and my head is everywhere.

As I saw, Deb's lips are moving. I did the polite thing and chucked in the odd "Oh really" and "Oh yeah. That sucks."

With Deb now sorted, I started to think back to when all of this shit started. Oh yeah, that is right. It all started when my bloody roster changed from three and one to a two and one.

This is the number of weeks in a rotation. Three weeks at work and one week at home. Now it is two weeks at work and one week at home. With a bit of a pay cut chucked on top, but whatever, that has nothing really to do with the story, I thought I would throw that in.

Well, here is the story. Once upon a time, I was at a mining camp. The day started just like any other day at a mining camp. With the alarm going off at 4 am "Beep, beep, beep."

"Oh shut up," I say to my alarm. I had placed it further than arms reach so that I cannot reach the snooze button. If you have a problem with getting up in the morning, you should try it.

That annoying beeping is hard to snooze through when you cannot reach it from your bed, and you have to get up to turn it off. Once you are up, you might as well stay up and get ready for work.

The usual morning routine, I turn the TV on for some background noise and head straight for the shower. Once I am dried. I put on my hi-vis pants and long sleeve shirt. Then the old steel cap boots. The whole time I hear info commercials in the background trying to sell me the latest Ab King Pro or Ab Swing or Ab Curl thing.

I brush my teeth, and it's time to leave my little donga. A donga is a small room usually three by three meters with a king-single bed, ensuite, wardrobe, mini-fridge, a desk, and a much-needed air conditioner as it's usually stinking hot. Every donga looks pretty much the same in every mining camp.

I make my way down the walkway to the dry mess. The dry mess is a fully staffed kitchen, with a hot and cold buffet; it is where we have our breakfast and dinner. We also make our lunches and grab our snacks for the day.

God, I did not realise how many notes I would have to make for the non-miner people who may be reading this book right now. Hello, by the way, thanks for buying the book. If I sell enough copies, I might be able to stop doing FIFO and start having lots of sleep in's. Ahh…, sleep.

Anyway, back to the story, I was walking down the walkway to the dry mess. I spotted my mate Dazza and said a cheery "Morning." He replied, "Morning." From the tone in his voice, I could hear something was wrong with Dazza. I asked, "What's wrong with you?"

"Bloody Christina," he groaned, "since her Dad died, she reckons her mum is lonely, and now she wants her to move into our place, with us."

"Oh yeah, that sucks," I agreed.

"Too right it does," he started up. "I only just got the last of the kids out the door, and I have become quite accustomed to walking around the house naked. If she moves in, I will have to keep my bloody clothes on. And the room I was going to turn into my Peter Brook memorabilia room will instead become that old hairy legged dragon's bedroom."

"Oh yeah, well that would suck, big time!"

We arrive at the dry mess, go through the turnstiles and say our goodbyes.

"Have a good one, Dazza."

"Yeah, you too Mick."

He appeared to be in a better mood after our chat, sometimes just offloading your frustrations to a mate helps.

If you have not been into a dry mess before, imagine a big, not flash restaurant. Probably the closest thing would be a Chinese restaurant but without all of the Chinese symbols. As you walk in, there is a hot buffet in front of you with a couple of cooks behind it making omelettes to order. At night you can order steak or fish, it is cooked fresh however you like it. At every mine site in Australia, Friday night is fish and chip night.

There is also a connecting dining room with plain looking tables and chairs. In this room, there is a cold buffet with a selection of pre-sliced meats, cheese, salads, fresh cut up fruit, dried fruit and nuts, whole fruit usually apples and bananas, cereals, yoghurt, sliced bread, rolls, wraps, cakes and biscuits. And worst of all, a Mrs Mac's pies and sausage rolls fridge. There is always one of these fridges. Beware, eating too many pies, and sausage rolls will make you fat. Trust me.

So, I order myself a large omelette with the lot, while it's cooking I cruise over to the cold buffet to make my lunch. I make a couple of ham and salad rolls, grab a couple of apples and to top it off, I grab a sausage roll. I know, and that is how I know it makes you fat.

Thanks to the Mrs Mac's fridge, I now have the starting of my very own muffin top. I have gone up a pants size since I started FIFO. Thanks to my genetics I am still slim compared to most of the guys and girls here.

I grab my omelette while thanking the cook. I make my way over to my usual table. I notice that Thailand Tim and Bob are already seated there. Thailand Tim's real name is Jarrod, but he goes to Bangkok that often that everyone calls him Thailand. Why Tim? Well, I guess it starts with T just like Thailand. Bob, well his real name is Robert. For some reason, people named Robert call themselves Bob and no one bats an eyelid. It makes entirely no sense to me though. You think it would be just Robert, Rob, Robbo or even Bert. Not, Bob.

I sit down with my large omelette and hear that Tim is having a dig at Bob.

"What's going on?" I asked.

"Hey Mick," Tim replies, "I was just telling Bob here, that he's an idiot."

"Oh okay, why's that?" I questioned.

"Go on Bob, tell Mick what you just told me," Tim said staring straight at Bob.

Bob reluctantly replied, "Oh my god, all I said was that I think I am in love with Joy."

Joy is the bar girl Bob met when he went to Bangkok with Tim last year. Oh, and Joy is 20 years old and about 50 kgs. Bob is over 50 years old and about 100 kgs. I know 100 kgs does not sound like much, but he is only 5 foot 4 and mostly stomach.

"And I told you, she probably has three or four other suckers just like you in love with her, and they would be sending her money over every month." With a sheepish look on Bob's face, Tim barked, "Oh no, you're not sending her money are you?"

"How did you know I was sending her money?" defensively Bob continued, "anyway, her mother is sick, and I do not want her working in a bar anymore. She promised me if I sent her over a couple of hundred dollars each month she would quit working the bar."

"Haha, see you are an idiot," laughed Tim.

 I have to admit, I agreed with Tim on this one. I have heard about this scam a couple of times before.

I sat back and enjoyed my omelette all the while listening to these two numbnuts debating the rules of the Thailand bar girls. Tim looks at me, sitting back in his chair and concluded their debate with saying, "There are so many different money making opportunities available to these girls, and it is all thanks to the lonely, horny, and cashed up Australian FIFO workers."

After breakfast, we all catch the bus to the mine site. Some people sleep, others play games or scroll through Facebook on their phones. Remember it is still only 5 am and dark outside.

I send Bec a "Have a great day. Love you," message. Oh, I have not mentioned Bec yet. I am married, and her name is Bec. Her real name is Rebecca, but you know us Aussies we have to shorten everything. Bec and I are what you would call high school sweethearts. I might as well go back even further and tell you how we first met.

We first met in high school in Year 8, but it was not until Year 10 that we finally got together. It was at my mate's Colin's birthday party. He always had the best parties. His parents had 20 acres of land, and we would go out to their big shed and get plastered. Colin was one of the popular kids at school. That was mainly due to him being a Year 10 who was dating a Year 12, her name was Sheree, he was always bragging about how they had sex here, and they did that there. It did backfire on him though. She got pregnant and with her parents, being the religious type made her have the baby. Colin finished up Year 10 and had to get himself a job. I saw on Facebook that they are still together and have four kids now. I couldn't help but notice that they both looked drained, and a lot older than what they are.

Back to Bec, a group of us were playing drinking games. As you do when you are that age, it was Truth or Dare. Colin dared me to ride one of the sheep in the paddock.

"Bring it on," I said. I thought how hard could it be there are people riding bulls, and this is just a little fluffy sheep.

Colin found a torch, and we all walked over to one of the paddocks. There were about fifteen of us kids. Colin shone the touch around the paddock until he found a sheep.

"Slowly sneak up behind it and grab the wool behind its head, then jump on its back, and it will take you for a ride," Colin saw I was looking a bit uncertain, he added, "Don't worry, my brothers and I do it all the time." I later found out that was a total lie, Colin and his brothers had never even tried it, not even once.

I climbed over the fence and snuck up to the sheep. It was a lot bigger than I had initially thought. I turned around, and looked towards the crowd; I pumped my fist up into the air. I guess I thought that would make me look cool or something. The group gave me a big cheer.

I turned back and walked towards the big sheep. Well, I thought, it is now or never. I leaned forward and grabbed two big handfuls of wool. Suddenly, the sheep threw its head around and stared straight into my eyes. It must have thought I was trying to hurt it because just like lightning it jumped up on all fours and started running, dragging me behind it. I somehow managed to pull myself up onto its back. Any sane person would have let go, but in my drunken state, I held on tighter.

I could hear laughter coming from every direction. In reality, it was only coming from one spot. The sheep in its scared state had decided to spin around in circles, which meant I was I spinning around in circles. I started feeling very sick. Oh no! I felt all of the alcohol and sausages that I had earlier coming up, and it did, all over the sheep and me. The sheep must have thought, stuff this for a joke. Wanting me off its back, it decided to bolt straight for the crowd of kids. Luckily, the kids had a fence to protect them from the sheep. Unlucky for the sheep and me though, we went head first into the fence.

The laughter was deafening. The sheep got up and staggered off, I tried to stand up, but I kept falling down. I blanked out a couple of times, coming to realise the laughter had stopped entirely. Colin's Dad had come from nowhere and didn't seem too happy about the situation. He managed to lift me up over the fence while saying. "You are coming with me you idiot and you lot, either go home or get in your sleeping bags and go to sleep," I thought I was in big trouble.

I was relieved to see that Bec was coming with us. We got into Colin's Dad's car, and he drove to the hospital.

Next thing I knew we were in the emergency department. When I had hit my head, I had split it open. I guess that would explain all of the dried blood on my shirt and neck. Bec held my hand and kept reassuring me that everything would be all right. It was all a bit of a blur. I ended up with 20 stitches to the top of my head and a big bald spot where they had to shave it.

At least mum had enough sense to make me shave my whole head, so I ended up looking like a Romper Stomper from that Russel Crowe movie instead of an old balding man.

After that, Bec and I were inseparable. God, if she could put up with me looking like that, then I had myself a keeper. She was a great kisser too. I did not want to know how she became so good at that though.

So there you have it a real romance story. I might as well keep going from here. After high school, Bec went on to study nursing, and I had many different jobs. I worked at the local super-mart in the fruit and veg section. I was a bottle shop attendant, a brickies labourer and I even installed Colorbond fencing for a while.

We then decided we wanted the great Australian dream, to buy a house together, however with my wages and Bec studying full time. The bank told us "You're dreaming," just like on that famous Australian movie, The Castle.

I tried the old working two jobs at once trick. This gave me no time off and made me very tired and very grumpy all of the time.

Then one day, I saw Johnno driving a brand new HSV Commodore. Johnno and I went to school together.

"Hey Johnno, what the hell?" I said while pointing at the car. "Are you a drug dealer or something?"

Johnno laughed "Na mate, I got myself a job in the mines doing FIFO. I'm on the blast crew."

"Okay, so what is FIFO and what is the blast crew?" I asked.

"FIFO means you have to fly into the middle of nowhere for 3 or so weeks then fly home and have a week off and you come back cashed up. The blast crew blows the ground up, and then the earth moving machines come in and dig it up."

"That sounds good. Any chance you can get me a job doing that?"

"I probably could. I will have to ask my supervisor and see what he says."

"That would be awesome. Thanks, Johnno."

"No worries. Hey, I have to go. I am meeting up with a couple of chicks I met off the internet. I hope that when they see me driving this beast, their panties will fall off, haha," he laughed.

"Alright have fun," I said.

Johnno cranked his stereo and did a massive burnout. I would later come to realise Johnno was the exact definition of a CUB or a Cashed-up Bogan, with his V8 commodore and ACDC cranking from an overpriced stereo. Not that there is anything wrong with being a CUB. That is what he is.

I went straight over to Bec's, parent's house, where she was still living, and I told her all about this FIFO thing.

"I will miss you, but if you just do it for a year or two, we should have enough for a house deposit. Then you can leave and get a regular job. I will be a qualified nurse by then so we will be able to make it work, and we can have our own home. Yay! Let's do it."

It was about a week later when I got the phone call.

"Hello," I said.

"Mick, it's me Johnno. How are you going?"

"Hi, yeah good thanks. How did you go?"

"Oh that. Yeah great. As soon as the girls saw me rock up in my new car, they were gagging for it. I bought them a carton of vodka cruisers, and we drove around town for a while until they were pissed as parrots and then we went back to mine and got it on like animals. They both had those tramp stamps and piercings."

"Hey Johnno," I asked. Trying to stop him going on with his story.

"Yeah."

"I was referring to the job. How did you go with getting me a job with you?"

"Oh that. Yeah well, Pete, my supervisor said we have enough blast crew, but if you want a job in the catering department until a job with us becomes available, he can probably get you one. What do you reckon?"

"Yeah, that sounds great. Thanks Johnno."

"No worries. I will tell Pete, and he will sort it out for you. See ya Mick."

"Thanks Johnno. See ya mate."

Woohoo, I am doing FIFO, I am doing FIFO. I will be jet setting around Australia, like a rock star.

Two weeks later and I was on my way to the airport.

Bec was driving and saying "I can't believe people get up this early. Keep an eye out for a Macca's I need another coffee."

We found a Mac Donald's and both ordered a sausage and egg, mac muffin meal with the hash brown and a coffee. We ate them while driving the rest of the way to the airport. I must admit I was feeling excited and nervous. I had only flown once, and that was to Bali on a family holiday when I was about five years old.

"Enjoy Port Hedland. Wherever that is," Bec said before giving me a big kiss and then driving off.

I checked in my bag and got my ticket. I then made my way up to the departure area. The airport was quite busy for such an early time in the morning. People were getting their coffees and take away sandwiches. Others were looking at magazines, and some were asleep on the benches. You could easily tell which ones were the FIFO workers, wearing there bright yellow and blue or orange and blue hi-vis shirts.

I found the Port Hedland gate and realised they were already boarding. Gee, that was good timing. I boarded and found my seat. Oh cool, it is a window seat. I buckled myself in and started to relax.

I was just about to fall asleep when I felt a presence next to me. I looked up and towering over me was the biggest Maori guy I had ever seen. He looked like he played for the New Zealand All Blacks. He was wearing an All Blacks supporter's top and was covered in those tribal tattoos that many of those Maori guys have. I think they have something to do with their family tree.

"Hey Bro, it's your lucky day. I'm seating next to you," the man mountain said as he squeezed into his and half of my seat pushing me almost through the window.

"Hey Bro, can you do me a favour and wake me up when breakfast is coming."

"Yep, sure thing," I said.

I started to think about how cool it would be to be that big. I reckon he could probably pick up a car, a little car, possibly a mini cooper. But then again he most likely could not sleep in a regular sized bed. He probably has a king size bed and sleeps diagonally or something.

"Hey Bro, stop staring at me," he said.

Oh shit, I did not realise when I was thinking, I was staring at him.

"Oh sorry," I said and turned away.

"Hey you're not a homo, are you? If you are, you do not have a chance with me, Bro. I am all about the ladies, and the ladies are all about me. Haha," he said.

"Haha. No, I have a girlfriend. Her name is Bec," I replied hoping to reassure him that I was straight. This big scary looking guy has one of those laughs that instantly put you at ease and makes you laugh.

"Well, that's good. I am George."

"I'm Mick."

"Why are you heading to Port Hedland?"

"I am going to work on the mine site in the catering department."

"Good for you. I operate the dozer on the mine. If this is your first time on a mine site follow me and I will show you where to go."

"Awesome. Thanks."

"No worries and remember don't stare at me it's weird. Haha."

"Haha I won't," I replied. Then I sat back, relaxed and started to wonder what a dozer is.

I must have fallen asleep as the next thing I knew we were landing and right to his word, George showed me where to go. We caught the company bus and started cruising down the main road towards the mine. It was amazing there was nothing for as far as the eye could see except red dirt, low shrubs and the odd dead kangaroo on the side of the road.

It took about an hour before we finally arrived at the camp. I do not know what I had expected. I probably should have done some research or at least ask Johnno some questions.

What I saw was a village made out of transportable buildings and a big red dirt car park, filled with white four-wheel drive vehicles with orange flashing lights on their roofs and hi-vis number stickers on their sides like, LV325.

There was the odd garden bed, which was an attempt at prettying up the place. There was also a swimming pool and a tennis court. The swimming pool would defiantly be a bonus during summer. It was only spring, and it was already boiling. I could just imagine how hot this place would get during the summer.

"Home sweet home, Bro," George said while placing one of his massive bear paws on my shoulder. "See that building over there, that is the village admin office, and that is where your boss will be. I have to go and get ready for work, have fun," he said as he walked off.

I walked through the dusty red carpark and into the site admin office.

"Hi, can I help you?" said the stocky woman behind the counter.

"Hi, yes, I'm Mick. I am supposed to start work here today."

"Oh yes. Hi Mick, I am Sandra. Nice to meet you," she said, "Let me have a look," as she typed something into the computer. "Here you are. I have you down for room cleaning. Come with me, and I will give you a tour."

I followed her back outside. The tour did not take too long. There was the dry mess, which I explained to you earlier. The wet mess, which is the pub, it looks like a big shed with a bar, some TVs up on the walls, three pool tables and lots of fans. There was also the swimming pool, tennis court, and some storage rooms and laundries, which look like a laundry mat with about six washing machines and six dryers. Lastly, there were heaps of dongas, which is what I would be cleaning. Sandra took out a key and opened up one of the dongas.

"This one is yours. Get changed and meet me back at the office, and I'll show you what you have to do."

"Cheers," I said as I walked inside the little room. I watched a documentary once about a minimum-security prison. You know one of those prison farms, and I am sure those rooms on that documentary looked precisely like this one. Anyway, I am here now, so I got changed into my new uniform and headed back towards the office.

"Arrr" I screamed. It sounded more like a 12-year-old girl's scream. I jumped back fearing for my life. Right there in front of me was a dragon. Well, a lizard on steroids anyway. This thing was massive. I have seen dogs smaller than this thing. I reckon this lizard could probably eat a whole dog easy.

Sandra came out of the office. "Oi, shut up people are trying to sleep. What are you screaming like a little girl about?"

I pointed down towards the dragon.

"Oh my god, it's just a bungarra. Just walk around it and don't you dare hurt it or it will be your job."

Me, hurt it? How could I do that? I think that dinosaur would tear me to shreds if I even got close to it. I walked around it staying at a very safe distance. I did not want it to feel threatened by me what so ever.

"Haha," Sandra started to lose it laughing. "Haha don't worry about them. You will get used to them and the snakes. It is the drop bears; you have to look out for, haha. Now come on. Grab that trolley and clipboard, and I will show you how to clean a room."

The trolley contains clean sheets, towels, floor mats, soaps, a broom, and a mop with its bucket. We went to a room marked on the clipboard as empty.

"Never trust the clipboard. Always knock first. You wouldn't believe the things I have walked in on,"

Sandra said. Therefore, we knocked on the door. No answer. We entered and started cleaning the room. We changed the sheets, and swapped the towels and floor mat over with fresh ones and lastly mopped the floor.

"Easy yeah? You have a map on the back of the clipboard for if you get lost and if you need anything I will be in the office," Sandra said and then she turned and walked away.

Easy enough, I thought and set about cleaning the rooms marked on the clipboard. I wonder what sights Sandra had seen by not knocking on the doors. I guess I would find out if I do not knock.

The next four rooms were pretty smooth and uneventful; the fifth room was a different story. I had started cleaning it just like the other rooms. However, there is supposed to be two towels per room, and there was only one hanging up in the bathroom. I looked around and saw that the towel was under the bed.

There you are I thought. I picked it up with my bare hand and noticed that it was crusty with a dry whitish powder on it. With the towel still in my hand, I looked further under the bed, and see a stack of porno magazines. I looked back at the towel, and it took a millisecond before it clicked in my head and I threw the towel across the room. Yuk, Yuk. I could not believe I had just picked up some other blokes wank rag. I felt like throwing up. I quickly went into the bathroom and washed my hands. I went through the whole cake of soap I did not care about wasting the soap. I did not want some other bloke's semen on my hands, Yuk. Once I was convinced that my hands were thoroughly clean, I went to the office to tell Sandra.

"Men are pigs Mick. You should know that you are a man. Now harden up and clean that room.

There are gloves in the storeroom. Now go and get a pair and while you are at it grow a pair," Sandra said.

Wow! I did not expect that response, I am used to women being a lot more, I do not know girly I guess. Sandra is a lot manlier than I am used to that is for sure. I wonder if all of the women that do FIFO are as rough as Sandra. I guess I will find out.

I got some gloves and sorted out the wank rag, I mean towel. The rest of the day went smoothly, and it was over before I knew it.

I went into the dry mess for some dinner, and it was a sea of hi-vis. I grabbed a plate full of roast beef and veggies and looked around for somewhere to sit.

"Hey, Bro, Mick come and sit with us," George called out from his table. It was full of the rest of the All Blacks team. As soon as I sat down, it started.

"Everyone this is Mick and Mick is gay."

"What the? No I'm not."

"Of course you are. Remember how you were staring at me on the plane."

"What? I have a girlfriend."

"Of course you do. What was her name again Brad or something."

"What? No, it is Bec, and she's a girl."

"Sure she is. Haha."

The whole table was pissing themselves laughing, I turned bright red, and I was trying very hard to think of what to say next. I took too long thinking.

"Nice come back Mick, Haha. Do not worry I am just messing with you. You have to be a lot quicker than that if you are going to survive this FIFO game. Haha."

That was my introduction to the mining sense of humour, which is taking the piss out of each other until someone does not have a comeback, and that means the other person won.

I must say it was a fun dinner listening to this lot taking the piss out of each other. They were all very skillful in the craft. I finished my meal and got up to leave.

"Hey Mick, you will have to come down and have some drinks with us on shift change," George said.

I was about to ask what shift change was but quickly stopped myself. I did not want to give these guys anything else to take the piss out of me with. I just said, "Sounds good."

I walked back to my room and called up Bec.

"Hi beautiful," I said.

"Hi Mick, how was your first day?" Bec asked.

I spent the next half hour telling her everything that had happened.

"Oh wow, that sounds very different. You know if you don't like it you can always come home."

Just then, I heard Sandra's voice in my head saying "Harden up." "No, it's all good. I will give it a good go. Well, I had better get some sleep. Love you. Good night."

"Love you too. Good night."

The next two weeks went along pretty well. Many night shift workers are sleeping during the day, so you need to be quiet when cleaning the rooms.

I still came across the odd towel wank rag, but I learned just to give them a fresh one.

I saw George on the way into the dry mess for dinner.

"Hey, Mick are you coming to the wet mess for a beer?"

"Umm, I wasn't going to, I'm pretty knackered."

"Bro, it is shift change. You have to come down."

"Oh okay. Why not?"

"Good. See you down there."

I called Bec and had a shower. Then I walked through the red dusty car park, and past the twenty or so white four-wheel drive vehicles to the big shed that was the wet mess. I saw George and the other All Black players sitting at one table.

"Hi guys," I said.

"Hey Mick," they all said in their own way, either with a nod, a smile or just speaking it. I sat down at the long wooden outdoor table. You know the type that you would see at a park or a camping ground. The table was already half full of empty beer bottles.

"Bro, I reckon you should go and get your guitar. That's what we need right now," one of the guys said.

"Yeah, na. Not yet. I can't be bothered getting up."

"Whatever. I am going to message Tina and book her in for later, do you want me to book you in too?"

"Na Bro, I'm sweet."

"Oh crap," he blurted, Tina is fully booked, "I bet it is those bloody dodgy drillers. I guess it might be

Shirley's lucky night," he said, and he turned his head and looked at a fat chick who was wearing bike shorts and who had visible cellulite.

"Is that Tina that cleans the rooms like me that you are talking about?" I asked.

"Yeah and that's not all she cleans. Haha," He nudged the guy next to him to show him that he had just said something hilarious.

"I don't get it," I said

"Bro, she's a hooker. You know a prostitute."

"Really? She looks so normal."

"Haha. Yeah well, what did you expect a hooker to look like. Some anorexic drug addict with no teeth like the ones you see on TV? Haha."

"I guess I never really thought about it." With that, I got up and went to the toilet. I walked in and saw that the urinal was full, so I went into one of the stalls to do a pee. I looked around at all of the graffiti. There were drawings of penises, vaginas, and bumholes. This place sucks, with the sucks spelled sux. There were rude poems. This AFL team is the best, which was scribbled out, and somebody else put their team's name in its place. There were also full conversations. For a good time, Shirley's room is H 19. Someone else wrote no it is K 12. You should know, you are the chubby chaser, and on and on it went. There were spelling mistakes everywhere.

I finished my pee, and as I am washing my hands, I saw many blokes walking straight out without washing theirs. Mental note to self, if I see those guys later, don't shake their hand.

As I walked out of the bathroom, I bump straight into Shirley.

"Well hello, you must be new here. I am Shirley. What's your name?" Shirley said while looking me up and down as if I was a piece of meat that she was about to eat.

"Hi, I'm Mick. Excuse me I have just seen a mate of mine," I blurted out and almost ran over to Johnno. Whom I saw was watching the whole thing.

"Haha. I see you have met Shirley," Johnno said.

"Yeah, I thought she was going to eat me."

"Yeah well, she will if you let her. She has done heaps of the guys around here and shift change at the wet mess is her hunting ground. Haha."

"What no way. Who would have sex with her?"

"You would be surprised. There are many lonely, horny guys up here and add a lot of alcohol and voila some poor sucker is waking up next to a grizzly bear. Haha," he laughed. "Hey, do you want to do a line?"

"What, you mean drugs?"

"Umm, yeah. What else? I bring up some speed for shift change every swing and Pete over there brings up the ecstasy."

"Really, how do you get them past airport security?"

"That's easy. Just put them in your wallet."

"What about the police and their sniffer dogs?"

"Well if you don't look dodgy, why would they hassle you and if you see the dog coming your way, go to the bathroom, get some hand soap and pop the drugs up your bum. Then rub some of the soap around your bum hole and voila all the dog smells is hand wash."

"Wow, when you put it that way it sounds pretty easy."

"It is. Anyway come and meet the drill and blast guys." We walk over to a group of guys who look as if they came straight from work to the wet mess, as they are all still wearing their dirty uniforms.

"Hey guys this is my mate Mick."

"Hi Mick," they all said in their own way the same as the Maori guys had. Due to there being so many of them they had pushed, two of the wooden tables together and both were almost full of beer and bourbon cans. These guys were giving the Maori guys a run for their money in the drinking department.

I sat down at the table and started talking to one of the drillers named Corey, and he sounded like he had taken too much of Johnno's speed. He told me about how he was using the money he earnt from drilling to start up a winery with his brother.

"I bought the land last year, and my brother is setting up the grape vines as we speak. Next year we plan to build a beautiful restaurant overlooking a big dam and a separate wine tasting room, where customers can try, and purchase a bottle of our wine, as soon as the winery is profitable enough to support both my brother and me. I will give FIFO away."

It just goes to show you cannot judge a book by its cover. This driller in his dirty uniform, and who is high as a kite, could one day be a successful winery owner and be selling you a glass of Chenin Blanc and describing it's fruity aromas or if you are a red wine drinker maybe a glass of Shiraz and he could be suggesting what meat goes well with it.

The night was pretty fun, lots of drinking, storytelling, and the Maori guys finally had the guitar out and were singing along with that.

All of a sudden I heard lots of cheering and laughter coming from behind me. I turned to see what all the fuss was about and there was Terry, one of the fitters in his birthday suit running around the wet mess. A fitter is a mechanic for the earth moving machinery.

Anyway, Terry was running around starkers and yelling to everyone to come for a swim in the pool.

I will stop and let you know what Terry looks like because it is a sight. Terry was the hairiest man I had ever seen hairy back, chest, legs, pubic area. The only place there was no hair on his head, so he looked like a monkey with its head shaved.

He did a couple more laps of the wet mess and ran off into the darkness towards the pool. Seconds later, we heard a big bang.

Everyone got up and ran towards where the bang had come from. We all came to a standstill in front of the pool gate, and everyone started losing it laughing. There in front of us lying in a big hairy heap was Terry; he had ran straight into the pool gate and knocked himself out. Everyone kept laughing for another 10 seconds or so and then we all realised he still was not moving. We all stopped laughing.

One of the other fitters, Steve, who was a member of the emergency response team put him into the coma position and told others to call the site nurse to get the ambulance down there. Another guy was asked to find Terry some clothes.

I started to think back to when I had almost knocked myself out due to that stupid sheep.

I probably should not call the sheep stupid. I was the stupid one for jumping on its back. The unfortunate thing was trying to sleep. Then I came along and jumped on its back.

I came back to reality and realised I was rubbing the scar on the top of my head. I looked around to see if anyone was watching me, but no one was paying me any attention. They were either watching or helping Terry into a neck brace and onto a stretcher. I must have been daydreaming for a while because within that time someone had managed to find a pair of board shorts and put them on Terry.

I later found out this was not to protect his modesty but rather to protect his job. When they filled out the incident report, it said that he had tripped over and banged his head on the way into the swimming pool. The report said nothing about him being drunk or naked at the time of the incident.

After the ambulance came and took Terry away, I figured I might as well stumble back to my donga and pass out. I could not remember the last time I had drunk that much alcohol, and I was as pissed as a fart.

I woke up about lunchtime the following day feeling like crap. My head was pounding, and my mouth was as dry as Ayers rock. I went into the bathroom and skulled about a hundred litres of water, straight out of the tap. The only problem with that was I never ran the tap long enough, and the water was still warm. Oh no, that just made me sick, and then it came straight back up.

I aimed for the shower as I started to throw up and managed to get it all in there. This was good because all I had to do then was turn the shower on to wash the majority of it down the plughole. I stripped off and hopped into the shower and using my foot, I pushed the remaining spew down the hole.

Ahh, the water feels so good, I made it as cold as I could handle to snap me out of that horrible groggy feeling. Oh, I suddenly realised I had a couple of beers in the fridge. I left the shower running and using the bath mat under my feet, so I did not slip over. I shimmied out to the refrigerator and cracked it open. The light from the fridge was like the lights from heaven, and I could hear the angels harps playing as I saw the beers sitting there on the shelf as if I was in a beer commercial.

I grabbed a beer, cracked it open and took three big gulps. Ahh, beautiful. I used the bath mat to shimmy back into the shower with my beer. I stayed in there for ages, drinking my beer with the cold water flowing over me like a waterfall.

Wow, this is the best feeling ever. It almost made it worthwhile being hung over. I think I just invented the best hangover cure, by combining the hair of the dog meaning a beer with a cold shower. I think I will call it the Wet Dog or the Hair of the Wet Dog. Maybe I will leave the name for now.

I dried off and lay back on my bed, with my last beer. I clicked on the TV and found my choices were Days of our Lives, The Young and Restless, Oprah or an old Elvis movie. I decided on the Elvis movie and called Bec.

I told her all about the crazy night I had last night and about Terry, the bald monkey.

She told me, "If it gets too crazy just quit and come home."

"Na it is fun," I said. With that, we said our goodbyes and I grabbed a towel and headed for the pool. I had a bit of a beer buzz going which made me feel a little better.

I saw Terry and a couple of the other guys from last night already relaxing in the pool.

"Hey guys," I said.

"Hey Mick," they all replied in the own way.

"How's your head, Terry?"

"Yeah pretty sore ay," he answered, "If anyone asks, I was sober, and I tripped over on my way to go for a swim. That is how I bumped my head."

I think he was trying to wink at me, but because he had his sunglasses on, I could not see his eyes, he just looked like his face was having a spasm.

"Yeah, no worries," I said and jumped in for a swim. There was not too much conversation as everyone was hungover. At least I did not have to go to work tonight like these guys. The cleaners are day shift only. However, almost everyone else has to do night shift.

I hung out there for a while swimming and sunbaking. Then I went back to my room, got changed and went in for some dinner. I was starving by that stage.

I walked over to the hot buffet and got myself a big plate full of chicken curry and rice. I looked around and saw a spare seat with the drillers that I was talking to last night.

"Hey guys. Mind if I join you?"

"Yeah, sit down. We were talking about who Justin woke up next to this morning," said Pete.

Justin was one of the other drillers. There were probably about six of them on that crew.

"What, I thought you said you are married with kids?"

"I am, but what happens in camp stays in camp," he replied.

I looked around, and everyone at the table acted as if this was normal. So I just said "Fair enough. So who was it?"

"Shirley, haha," Pete laughed, "and that's not even the best bit. Go on tell him."

"Haha, when I realised it was Shirley next to me in bed. I was like Tom Cruise in one of those Mission Impossible movies. I had my arm under the pillow spooning her. I slowly pulled it out inch by inch. I was making sure that I did not wake her. Then I slowly rolled off the bed onto the floor and felt around for my clothes. Once I had them all, I made my way to the door in stealth mode. As I opened the door and the light came into the room, I realised it was my bloody room, not hers. Haha. Then I flicked on the light and said "Oi Shirley. Wake up," and she said "What?" and I said, "Hey can you please get your stuff and leave my room?" and what a champion, she just got dressed and left."

The whole table pissed themselves laughing. We were all so loud that everyone else in a mess turned around to see what we were laughing about and some of the drillers at the table even started humming the Mission Impossible theme song.

"Whoops. Look at the time. We have to go. See ya, Mick."

"Yep see ya guys."

They all grabbed their plates and left. I finished my dinner still picturing Justin acting like Tom

Cruise, just so he did not wake up the sleeping grizzly bear that is Shirley, pretty funny. I took my plate up to the dishwasher chick. That is one of the best benefits of FIFO, not having to wash your dishes. I went back to my room and watched a movie until I fell asleep.

The next week was uneventful. Breakfast, cleaning rooms, dinner, call Bec, sleep and repeat.

It was finally fly out day, "Yay" everyone was excited. We were all on the bus heading to the airport, and everyone was drinking. Then at the airport, everyone was drinking. Then on the plane, everyone was drinking. I was surprised by how much these guys and girls could drink.

I hope that none of these people were driving themselves home from the airport because if they were, they would blow over. The majority of them have come straight off nightshift, and if they did not have a sleep on the plane, they would be awake for over 24 hours before they get home.

I had Bec picking me up. I walked through the arrival area and saw her; you could not wipe the smile from my face. I went straight up to her and gave her the biggest hug and kiss.

"God, I'm glad to see you," I said.

"Yep me too."

"Let's get out of here."

As we were walking out, I saw Justin cuddling some woman, and she had a couple of kids with her. I guess they must be his wife and kids. Then I saw Shirley walking up. Oh no, I thought this is not going to go well. Shirley just walked straight past and into the arms of some other bloke and they kissed and walked off together. Wow, you do not see that every day do you. I did not say anything to Bec. I was just happy to be home.

We drove straight back to my place and went at it like rabbits. Well, it was quick like a rabbit. Give me a break; it has been three weeks with no action. I did try to hold back. I told Bec that I would get her next time. We cuddled up, and I fell asleep for half an hour or so, as guys do.

We stayed in bed for the next hour or so talking about everything. I told Bec about the Justin and Shirley thing, and she shared about the crazy things she sees at the hospital.

I checked my bank account and saw there was a couple of grand in there. Wow, there has not been that much money in my bank account for a long time. Well never actually. I took Bec out for a couple of nice dinners, bought myself a new PlayStation and her some jewelry. By the time the week was over, I had spent the lot.

Wow, it just goes to show how quickly it can all go when you are not paying attention to it. Bec and I decided if we were ever going to get a place of our own, we would need to be a lot smarter with the money that we earn. So we did up a budget, and if we stick to it, we will have a house deposit by next September.

It took us until the following February to get the deposit. Due to when your income goes up somehow so does your expenses. We found ourselves going out to eat a lot more, buying expensive gifts for each other and our family and friends. We would go to the movies instead of hiring a DVD or just watching Netflix. When we would go to the pub, we would shout our friends who did not earn as much as us.

I am jumping ahead a bit too quick. Let me backtrack. After that first swing, the next few swings, well really the next two years before I changed careers, were all the same. It was; breakfast, cleaning rooms, dinner, maybe a couple of drinks at the pub, call Bec, sleep repeat. Shift change was always fun, getting drunk and having Terry doing his nudie runs. He did these almost every shift change. He just learned to slow down before he got to the pool gate if he was going for a swim.

Let me think. There were funny and exciting things that did happen during those two years. All right, here is one I found interesting and I think you would too.

I was cleaning the rooms as usual, when.

"Hey Mick," it was Sandra calling out from behind me, as she made her way towards me.

"Yeah, what's up?" I replied

"I need you to go to room G 12 and pack it up. The bloke missed the plane, and when they finally got in touch with him, they were told he was going back to prison for attempted murder."

"Oh okay."

"Yeah I know right. Anyway, you know where the boxes are. Just give it a good clean and let me know when you have finished so I can update the room's availability on my computer."

With that, she walked off, and I went to the storeroom and grabbed some packing boxes. I took them over to G 12 and opened up the door. I was wondering whose room it was.

My question was answered as soon as I walked through the doorway. On a shelf next to the TV was a photo of a huge scary looking guy covered in tattoos with an older lady. Probably his mum, I recognised the bloke as one of the crusher guys. I did not know his name. He was probably about the same size as George. I wonder who would win out of a fight between those two; I could picture the fight now.

This is the main event of the evening, in the super heavyweight division. Fighting out, of the blue corner, standing six feet five inches tall weighing in at 300 pounds, George the Massive Maori and fighting out of the red corner standing six feet four inches tall weighing in at 305 pounds, Scary Old Mate from the crusher. The crowd goes wild.

Oh well, enough daydreaming I had better start packing away his stuff. There was not much in the room. I put some of his work uniforms on the bottom of the first box and then placed his small TV and DVD player on top. Next were his photos, toiletries and all of his protein powders. Lastly, I was going to finish the box off with the rest of his clothes. I opened up the drawers next to his bed and "What the?" it was chock a block full of women's silk underwear. There were lots of different knickers and bra combinations. I had heard of guys keeping souvenirs after having slept with a chick, but this was ridiculous, and they were all large. Old Mate fancied the bigger girls. I put them all into the box and then I realised there was no men's underwear. I took a closer look at the sizes on the women's underwear, and they were all the same size and large enough to fit Old Mate. BOOM! The guy is a cross-dresser or whatever you call a guy that wears women's underwear. His scary factor just went down by half.

I went to the office and told Sandra.

"That's pretty funny. I would not go around telling anyone else if I were you, it could be your job. And considering that he is going to jail for attempted murder, if it gets out that you told everyone his little secret, it could cost you your life."

I suddenly felt sick, his scary factor just jumped back up a thousand points. I went back to the room and finished packing the boxes and cleaned the room. I never did tell anyone about that guy, not even Bec. Until now anyway but I am sure that you can keep a secret.

I feel comfortable that you have been entertained enough for those two years and we can now jump forward to us building our dream home.

It's February, and we have our house deposit, Yay. Bec is working full time as a registered nurse, which means with having two incomes and the deposit we can finally get a home loan. We visited a couple of new estates and decided on one not too far from the beach that had plenty of parks close by for when we eventually have kids.

We found an impressive display home, four bedrooms, two bathrooms, study, and theatre room, with all the bells and whistles. Life was good.

While the house was under construction, I got the opportunity to leave room cleaning and get trained up on the dump trucks. I was excited that I would be sitting in an air-conditioned cab and not having to push a room cleaning trolley around in the heat while shooing away flies at the same time.

I hopped on the bus with George and all of the other machinery operators and headed into the mine site. I had seen pictures of the massive machines before, but it's not until you see them in real life that you realise how huge they really are.

When I arrived, I was introduced to Trish, the truck trainer. I was to spend the next three weeks with her doing powerpoint presentations, paperwork and learning how to operate the dump truck. I found out that Trish was my old boss Sandra's girlfriend. What a spin out I did not even realise Sandra was a lesbian.

Anyway, when Trish took me over to see one of the dump trucks, I was amazed at how big it really was. I could not touch the top of the tyre even if I jumped.

When we got into the cab, I sat in the driver's seat; it felt like I was sitting on a balcony of a two-story house it was up that high off the ground. I was also surprised that the truck had an automatic gearbox. I had expected some complicated gearbox system with lots of gears. The braking system took a while to get used to. There was the standard brake on the floor the same as the one everyone has in his or her car. However, you can only use that one under 10 km/hr. If you use it over that speed, the brakes scream at you. The trucks standard brake that you use the majority of the time is a lever on the right-hand side of the steering wheel which is called a retarder. You pull it down, and the truck slows down. There is also a park brake switch, and a secondary brake, that is the foot pedal on the left side that you push down if all of the other brakes fail. So there you have it four brakes.

It was fun driving this massive machine around. What is funny though, is that you get used to the size of it a lot quicker than you thought you would. This is because everything is in proportion, the roads are wider, and the parking spaces are bigger.

By the end of the three weeks, I felt confident with driving the truck by myself. I had my week off and then two weeks of day shift driving the massive machine.

It was the sixth week of driving that was a challenge. It was night shift, I had never had to stay awake all night working before. Of course, I have been to parties where we stay up all night drinking and talking rubbish. This in no way compared.

At about 2 am your body wants to shut down and go to sleep. Your eyelids become so heavy it is hard to keep them open. I came close to hitting the high wall a couple of times. I had thought I had blinked but what happened was I had a micro-sleep. For this to make sense, a high wall is the wall of the big hole we drive up and down. A micro-sleep is when you think you just closed your eyes for half a second, and it turns out to be between one to twenty seconds, which is a long time to be driving with your eyes closed, especially when you are driving a 250-ton dump truck.

I did not want to tell the supervisor because I thought he might say, "I do not think you are cut out for this kind of work," and I would have to go back to room cleaning.

By the end of the shift, you are completely knackered. You fall asleep on the bus going back to camp. Then after breakfast, you are in your bed and asleep by 7 am, hoping to sleep until 4 pm. However, being daytime, your body says you should be awake so at midday you wake up and stare at the ceiling for the next four hours hoping to get back to sleep.

I asked some of the other operators what they do to stay awake, and there was a real mix of opinions. Some took sleeping pills to go to sleep and then at night No-Dozes, which are caffeine pills to keep awake. Others drank Red Bulls and lots of coffee. Some cranked up the heavy metal and techno music in their cabs, while the alternative people ate green apples and put peppermint oil on their necks, saying that the peppermint smell wakes you up. And then to put lavender oil on their pillows to put them to sleep sounds very hippy to me but if it works for them why not.

I struggled on night shift but I enjoyed driving the dump truck, and I enjoyed the pay increase, especially now that I had a mortgage. There were many operators, who did not like the trucks. They would say that the trucks are boring and you have too much time to think while you are in that little cab by yourself. They would overthink and find that they would end up becoming depressed, especially if there was stuff going on back home, and they were too far away to do anything about it.

I remember it became too much for Sam. He told me one day that his wife was divorcing him and going for full custody of the kids. The full custody bit was so he would have to pay more in child support. At the time, he was only allowed to have supervised visits with his kids because she had put a restraining order on him. He swore he never touched her and believed it was her lawyer who had advised her to do this making it easier for her to get full custody. Poor Bugger.

Well, one day Sam did not show up for work. The supervisor went to his room to check on him, only to find Sam dead. He committed suicide by overdosing on pills washing them down with a lot of alcohol.

I guess the "harden up" approach we have in mining does not always work. The ex-wife did get the full custody she had wanted, but without the huge child support check, she had expected to get from Sam to raise the kids.

That supervisor was never the same either. How could you be after seeing the dead body of one of your workmates? He quit mining a month later, and I do not think he ever stepped foot back on a mine site.

I know stories like that can be a bit depressing, so let me bring the happiness level back up a couple of points.

Our house is finished. Yay! I unlocked the front door for the first time and said to Bec.

"Honey we're home," we laughed and then I said, "come here. I want to pick you up and carry you over the threshold like they do in the movies."

"Oh, you are such a romantic," She laughed.

I picked her up and God, she was a lot heavier than I had thought; I almost dropped her as I carried her through the doorway. I set her back down, and as she was standing there looking around, I dropped to one knee and pulled a ring out of my board shorts pocket.

"Hey Bec, turn around."

"Yeah what," she said while turning around. She looked at me holding the ring. "Yes, yes, yes, I will marry you."

"I haven't asked you yet."

"Oh sorry. Well, go on then."

"Bec you are the love of my life. I want to be with you forever, and have children with you and grow old with you. Will you marry me?"

"Yes, yes. Of course, I will," I put the ring on her finger, and she said, "You know what?"

"What?"

"I knew you were going to ask me."

"Oh yeah and how did you know that?"

"Because when we were at the servo, and you were fuelling up the car. I opened the glove box to get out a new CD and I found the ring and the bit of paper with your little speech on it asking me to marry you."

"Wow! Way to kill the moment Bec," I thought to myself.

We waited another year, and then we got married. The wedding was down South at a beautiful winery. Bec looked stunning in her white dress, and I wore a matching white suit. I thought I looked pretty cool. George and Johnno came, and we all got drunk together and danced up a storm. It was great to be married to the love of my life, have an excellent job and be living in our dream home. Life is great!

The following year was uneventful. We had settled into married life, and life had become routine. I would fly up to work for the three weeks, and we would talk on the phone, then I would be home for a week. She was still working her regular shifts when I had my week off. We did not see each other very much, we would go to the movies and out for dinner together when we could.

I had a lot of free time, so I started gaming online. I found it entertaining, as you can play with people from all over the world. It made the week off fly fast.

I was back at work making myself a coffee before our pre-start meeting when I heard a familiar voice from behind me.

"Hey Mick," said Kev.

"Hey Kev," I replied.

"How was your break? Get up to anything interesting?"

"Yeah, pretty good thanks. I took Bec out to dinner a couple of times, did some gaming. What about you?"

"Yeah, not bad. I took the boat out a couple of times and caught some good size snapper."

I have to interrupt the conversation and tell you Kev's nickname, it is Nappy Pants. I do not say it to his face because he hates it, but others do, and he had threatened to report them to HR for bullying and get them sacked.

Kev got the name when he was a driller. He operates the excavator now but back then, we had a seafood night at the dry mess, and the oysters he ate did not agree with him. A couple of hours into the shift, Kev had to call up his supervisor to be picked up in a light vehicle, for a code brown which means he needs to do a poo in the toilet.

There are no toilets in the pit where the drillers drill. If they are busting to relieve themselves, they have to be picked up in a light vehicle and taken up to the toilet. Most wait until their smoko or lunch break.

Anyway, Kev only made it halfway out of the pit before he farted and shat himself. The smell was that bad, the supervisor told him to take the car back to camp and have the rest of the night off and to leave the windows down in the light vehicle overnight to air it out.

Kev drove all the way back to camp in his filth. Hence, the name Nappy Pants. You would think he would have just chucked his undies and wiped his butt in the toilets at the crib hut, before driving the 20 minutes back to camp. I guess Kev wasn't exactly the sharpest tool in the shed.

Anyway, Nappy-Pants and I took our coffees into the pre-start room and listened to our supervisor do his return to work speech.

"Hi everyone. Welcome back. I hope you all had a good break. We will be digging here blah, blah, blah and tipping there blah, blah, blah. Also, I know there have been rumors goh ing around that we might be changing our roster to a two and one and well, yes the stories are true, and as of right now we are on a two and one. I know there will be some moaning about the slight drop in pay. There will also be some happy people with the ability to spend more time at home. Regardless of how you feel this has come straight from management, and there is nothing I can do to change it. So do not come up and whinge to me about it. Anyway, any questions that do not relate to the roster change? Nope! Good, go to work then."

"Sweet, two and one. I'll be able to do heaps of fishing," said Kev.

"Yeah sounds great. I cannot wait to tell Bec. She'll be stocked."

"Hey, you know what you should do. You should surprise Bec. Just do not tell her. Then rock up with some flowers and be like, surprise."

"That's a brilliant idea, Kev. That's exactly what I am going to do."

The next two weeks dragged. I could not wait to get back home and surprise Bec.

It was now finally over, and I was on the plane flying back home. Yay!

As we touched down in Perth, I must admit I was very excited about surprising Bec. I have never been able to surprise her. She would always be like, I knew you were going to do this or that killing the mood instantly.

She could not know about this though. I only knew about it two weeks ago myself, and I played it cool on the phone as well. It was not very hard. These days the phone calls were almost precisely the same every day.

"Hey Bec. How was your day?"

"Yeah good thanks. How was yours?"

"Yeah good. What did you get up too?"

"Not much. I just finished at the hospital. I had to do bedpans and a couple of catheters. Now I am knackered. What about you?"

"I just drove the truck around and around in circles, while trying to stay awake. Same old, same old."

"Well, I had better get some sleep. Night."

"Yeah night."

I guess you could say we were in a bit of a rut. Everything seemed routine these days. I think that happens to everyone that has been together for as long as we have.

Our sex life had also been on the decline. We probably have sex once or twice a break, which on a three and one roster equals once or twice a month or twelve to twenty-four times a year. That is pathetic in anyone's books.

She once joked about having a threesome to spice things up. I thought about it for about 10 seconds. Some of the single guys at work had bragged about having them. That was with just random girls or their so-called girlfriends that they didn't really love or see a real future with.

I do not think you could do this with someone you love. There would be jealously and what if your girl started fancying girls and turned into a lesbian. Could I even satisfy two girls at the one time? Bec was the only girl I had been with, and I do not even know if I am doing that right. Call me old fashioned, but I think once you find the one, that is you for life. Na, I felt a threesome was not the way to go for us.

She then told me she was talking about two guys, not two girls and that took me 0 seconds to think about that. As if, I want to see some other guy having sex with my wife. No way, and what if the other guy tried to touch me? Yuk.

Sorry, I am not homophobic, but I have no interest in other guys. Terry's nudie runs on shift change are bad enough.

I told her no way, and she just said she was joking anyway. She had just wanted to get a reaction out of me. Phew. I was glad she was kidding about that.

Back to the surprise, I left the airport and drove straight to the florist; I ordered twenty-four roses. Thinking I was such a romantic until the shop assistant told me the price, and I quickly changed my order to a dozen roses. Gee whiz, I was not going to go broke, wasting my money on flowers.

I think a dozen roses would pretty much have the same effect as the twenty-four roses. God, I did not realise how expensive flowers could be.

Ahh, home sweet home, I thought as I pulled into the driveway. That is strange; there was a car parked there that I did not recognise. It must be the cleaner's car. Bec told me we have a cleaner pop in while I am at work. That would make sense why I did not know the vehicle.

I grabbed my dozen roses and snuck in the front door. I did not want to make any noise just yet. This is going to be the best surprise ever I could barely contain my excitement. I heard noises coming from the bedroom. She must be relaxing on our bed watching a movie. We had an excellent surround sound system, set up on the wall in front of our bed. We would spend plenty of time cuddled up watching movies on it.

As I got closer, I could hear moaning and sex noises. Oh my God, it sounds like Bec is watching porn. I never knew that she was into that kind of thing. I wonder if she has a vibrator. Some of the guys at work told me that they had bought ones for their wives and girlfriends and when I was a cleaner I would come across them from time to time. Shirley was the worst; she would leave hers out all of the time along with her porn DVDs.

I stopped at the door and wondered what would happen next. I pictured myself bursting through the door, and there Bec would be under the covers watching this movie. She would look up at me with my dozen red roses and be like, come to me, you romantic man. We would then go at it for ages and collapse in a pool of sweat.

With that thought in mind, I gripped the door handle and burst through the door with a massive smile on my face.

"What the hell?" I yelled in shock. What I saw in front of me, I could not even process. There on our bed. On mine and Bec's bed. The bed we bought together brand new when we first moved into this house, our house, our home.

There on the bed with my TV and surround sound system playing a porno was Bec and two random guys, fully naked going at it. In some position, I had not even thought was possible. I thought for a second, maybe she was being raped. I could not comprehend that Bec would voluntarily do something like this to me of her own free will. One look at her face and I could tell she had loved every minute of it until I had interrupted.

The shock must have worn off, and rage and adrenaline came through me. I leaped at the guys throwing punches and trying to rip them off her.

What happened next I had not expected. How can you expect anything when you are blindsided with what I have just walked into. Since I was the one that started throwing punches, the guys felt justified in throwing punches back at me and the fact that there were two of them and only one of me, they beat the crap out of me.

I could hear Bec yelling at them to stop and to leave me alone. Her yelling stopped them, but not straight away, a couple more punches and kicks, and I guess then, they felt like quitting.

With my one good eye, I watched from a heap on the floor as they grabbed their stuff. One went to kiss Bec on the cheek and told her that he would call her later after she had sorted that loser out.

"Just go, Dwayne," she replied. Staring at me in my sorry state, she began to cry. "What are you even doing here?" she asked while putting her underwear and a top on. The porno was still playing loudly in the background.

"My roster changed, and I wanted to surprise you," I answered still laying on the floor. I did not want to move. My ribs hurt like hell and I was finding it hard to breathe. God, could this get any worse?

"Hey Bec?" Dwayne had come back into the bedroom.

"What the hell are you still doing here?" Bec asked.

"Piss off," I managed to get out. I was so filled with rage; I wanted to kill this guy. How could someone do this to me? I know he does not know me, but he has to know she is married. There are photos of us all over the house. There is even our wedding photo on the bedside table. Was this guy looking at our wedding photo while having sex with my wife, just laughing at me? What is wrong with people? I could hear them talking again.

"I would go, if this idiot hadn't parked behind me, blocking me in."

"Oh okay. Where are your keys, Mick?"

I summoned up all of my strength and lunged at Dwayne. As I said, I wanted to kill him. Due to the beating both of the guys had given me he easily pushed me away with one hand.

"Stay down idiot, or I will beat your ass again."

"Leave him alone."

Bec reached into my board shorts pocket and grabbed my car keys. "I'll be right back," she said as she left with Dwayne.

Dwayne. What a dumb name. I know I am going to hate or dislike everyone with that name now.

They will be like "Hi, I'm Dwayne," and I will be like "Shut up Dwayne. You're a dick."

Bec came into the room. She started doing her whole nurse thing and checking for broken bones, cuts, and stuff.

"Does anything hurt?" she asked.

My heart you bitch, you horrible, horrible person you, where do you think it bloody hurts? I could hardly even talk. I was filled with rage, how could she do this to me? My emotions were going everywhere. I burst out crying; my whole body was shaking and moving about without my control. I had never felt so out of control of my own body and emotions before.

"You are just going through shock Mick. Everything will be okay. Just keep breathing, and I will be back in a sec. I am going to call an ambulance for you."

An ambulance, I am not that hurt, am I? Well, I must admit the adrenaline was wearing off, and I was starting to feel a lot more pain.

She came back into the room and turned off the porno that was still playing on the TV.

"So, what are you doing here?" she asked again.

"I told you my roster changed," I coughed up a little blood as I answered.

"Actually, on second thoughts, don't talk."

A couple of minutes passed in silence, and all I could see was Dwayne and his mate all over Bec.

There was a knock on the door, and a voice called out.

"Hello, Paramedic here, can we come in?"

"Yes, in the bedroom," Bec called back. She

introduced herself as a nurse and told them everything.

The paramedics gave me a green whistle to suck on, for the pain.

"Relax Mick, we are going to lift you onto the stretcher and take you to the hospital. Everything will be alright," one of the paramedics said.

"Do you want to ride in the back with him?" a paramedic asked Bec.

"No. Thank you. I will drive myself and meet you there."

By this stage, I did not want to look at her anyway. I hoped she crashed on the way to the hospital. At least then, she could feel part of the pain that I was feeling. Even with the green whistle, doing its thing, it was not taking the pain away from my heart.

I lay on the hospital bed awaiting my results. Earlier a doctor had examined me and had ordered some x-rays of my chest. Possible broken ribs, he had told me.

"Good news. Your ribs are not broken; they are just bruised. So once you are finished with the police, you will be fine to go home," the doctor said to me.

"Police, what police?" I asked.

"Oh, the nurses did not tell you, they are in the hallway. It is hospital policy that when a patient arrives in a state that suggests an assault, the police are contacted."

"Oh, okay. Thanks," I replied. Well, at least those two scumbags might get charged with assault and hopefully get some jail time. That would make me feel a little bit better.

"I will tell them to come in." With that, the doctor left the room, and the police officers entered.

"Good evening, I am Senior Constable Thomas, and this is Constable Harper, can you please tell us what happened to you?" Thomas was a powerful looking man in his early fifties, and Harper was a pretty lady in her early twenties. She looked fresh out of the academy. Anyway, I told the officers the whole story, and Harper took many notes.

After I had finished, Thomas said, "Being honest with you Michael, there will not be a lot that we can do to help you. This is because you have already admitted to us that you attacked them first. They will claim it was self-defense, even though it was excessive. Let us hope that they do not lay charges on you for assault." With that, the police officers said goodbye and left.

Put me up for assault, what the? I honestly do not think I even got one good hit on either of them. Bec was next to walk through the doorway.

"How are you feeling?" She asked.

"Yeah great, I have bruised ribs, thanks to your two boyfriends."

"It's your fault. You shouldn't have tried to fight the guys."

"You shouldn't have been having sex with them."

"Don't yell at me. You shouldn't have been there; you should have been at work."

"What. So this is my fault is it?"

"Well, it's not mine."

"Are you serious? What should I have done? Just walked in and asked the two random guys nicely.

Hey, excuse me, if it is not too much trouble, can you please stop having sexual intercourse with my wife and leave my house. Only if that is okay with you. I do not want to inconvenience you too much."

"No need to be a smart ass about it."

Just then a grumpy old nurse popped her head around the door. "Excuse me; can you two keep it down? There are other people in this hospital, and they don't need to listen to you two carrying on."

"Sorry. We will keep it down," Bec said. There was a silence for a bit. "I'm leaving you Mick. I have not been happy for a long time."

"What? This is the first time I am hearing about this."

"Listen to me. I've called your brother, and you can stay at his place for the week before you go back to work."

"You did what?"

"He will be here soon to pick you up."

"Is this because I said no to a threesome? I didn't want it to ruin our relationship, and I thought you said you were joking about that."

"Do you want to go there? I didn't want to bring this up but if that is what you want," she took a breath and carried on, "when we have sex, it is so fricken boring and routine I find myself faking an orgasm to make it hurry up and end. You do know there are more positions than just missionary don't you?"

"Oh my God, when did you turn into such a bitch? You are not the Bec I know, who are you?"

"Well, you would know me if you weren't so busy playing those stupid computer games all of the time. Who are you playing with anyway? What grown-up stays up until two in the morning playing these dumb games? Oh my god. Grow up."

"Bitch," it was all I could think of to say. I couldn't believe she felt this way about our relationship, sex life, and my gaming. All of my mates are gamers.

"Anyway, in regards to the house, I have had it appraised, and you can either buy me out, or I can buy you out. Alternatively, we can sell it. We should end up with five to ten thousand each, after fees."

"Oh my god. How long have you been planning this and don't you want to at least try to work it out?"

"I have tried, and I am tired of trying. I have to do me now. I am allowing myself to be happy. I am finally permitting myself to be happy."

"What the hell are you going on about?"

"I have been seeing someone Mick."

"No shit. Two someones I would say."

"No not them, they are just a bit of fun."

"Wow! Great I got beaten up just for a bit of fun."

"No, you got beaten up because you were trying to be a hero."

"Piss off."

"Anyway, I have been seeing a lady."

"What, so you are a lesbian as well?"

"No, but if I wanted to be that would be my choice and mine to make alone."

"Why are you talking like a bloody hippy?"

"I am trying to tell you, I have been seeing a lady. She is a life coach, and she told me you are holding me back. I have a fantastic future ahead of me, but before I can become the lioness I was born to be, I have to cleanse myself of all of the negative energy in my life. Mick, you are that negative energy."

We had a pause in the conversation as she locked eyes with me, I waited to see what she would say or do next. Honestly, I was starting to think I may just have dodged a bullet here. She was sounding like she was one step away from the looney bin and getting a free jacket, a straitjacket.

There was a bit more silence and then a knock on the door. It was my brother Shane.

"Hey mate. Hey Bec, are you ready to go?" he asked.

I looked at Bec. I mean, I really looked at Bec, her long brown hair, her face, her body and into her green eyes. The eyes I used to love looking into, the eyes that used to love looking into mine. She had changed. This woman staring back at me was not my Bec. The Bec I fell in love with and asked to marry me. The Bec I was so happy to build a home with and was hoping to create a family with, this Bec was a stranger to me. How had I not notice her change? It was not even a little change.

"Oi Mick, are we going? I have parked in a loading zone and if we get a ticket because you want to be a weirdo, staring into Bec's eyes. You are paying for it."

"Yeah stuff it. Let's go."

"See ya Bec."

"Bye Shane, Bye Mick."

I didn't say bye, stuff her, whoever she is, she doesn't deserve me saying goodbye. With that

Shane, and I walked out of the room, and I signed myself out of the hospital.

"You look like crap Mick."

"Thanks, I feel like crap too."

"So what happened?"

I told Shane the whole story.

"Hey, if you want me to get some mates together and find these guys, we will smash them for you. If that's what you want?"

"Na. Thanks anyway, I think if it were not these guys, it would have been another two guys."

"Well, let's get some pizza, and we can hang out and do some gaming."

"Sounds good to me."

See Bec, lots of grown-up men play computer games.

We arrived at Shane's place. It is not massive, just a one bedroom, one bathroom flat. Shane does not need anything too big or flash since it is only him living in it.

"You've got the couch Mick. I'm not giving up my bed just because you can't win a fight."

"Haha. Sounds fair."

That next week was pretty good considering how the week had started. We just hung out gaming and watching Netflix to all hours of the morning. Shane had to work during the day. He is a manager at Mc Donald's. Not a glamorous title but Shane had gotten a job there when he was a teenager and just never left. He was happy cruising through life and had no big dreams of becoming anything more, and that is not a bad thing. Not everyone has to have dreams of becoming a big CEO of a company, and from what I have heard; most of those guys are stressed out and eventually have a heart attack before they are fifty.

Well, the week was over, and I got Shane to drop me off at the airport on Tuesday morning. For some reason, FIFO workers always start their weeks around the middle of the week and not on Monday's like the rest of the world. Maybe the flights are cheaper? Perhaps they would lose too many of the party animal workers if they flew them back on the Sunday or Monday due to them failing drug tests.

"Hey thanks for letting me crash at yours."

"No worries. I guess you will want to stay next break too?"

"Yeah if that's cool?"

"Yeah no worries."

"Hey can you do me a massive favour and get my stuff from my house or Bec's house. Whoever's house it is now."

"Yeah no worries. Now get out of my car so that I can go back to bed."

"Haha. Yeah alright see ya." With that, I grabbed my bag and headed into the airport.

After checking in, I make my way up to the departure area and order a cappuccino. I see Deb, one of the wheel loader operators sitting by herself near the window watching the planes taking off and I make my way over to sit next to her.

"Hey Deb. Mind if I join you?"

"Hi Mick, grab a seat."

I quickly asked her how her break was. I did not exactly want to tell her or anyone about mine, and she loves talking about herself anyway.

"Yeah, it wasn't too bad," she started "my daughter Ashley has just turned 13, and the poor dear is going through puberty. Her hormones levels are going crazy, and this has, in turn, made her very moody. To be completely honest she is acting like a right little bitch. Excuse the language," I smiled and nodded my head for her to go on. And on and on she went. Blah, blah, blah, blah, blah.

Woo, woo, woo. Did you see what happened there? I am talking to you the reader, not Deb. Did you feel a little Deja vu? If not, go back to the start of the book and read the first couple of pages. Until you know what I am talking about.

Do you like what I did? We are back to where we started a full circle. Now you must admit that it was a beautiful piece of creative writing. Wasn't it? Well, I hope that you are enjoying the story so far. I am going to try something a little different for the next part of the book....

But first, you know what? I think you deserve a break. Go on get up, stretch your legs, go to the toilet, and grab something to eat or drink. Even have a play on Facebook or Instagram if you want and while you are there why not like the author's pages and send him a message telling him what you think of the story so far. The details are on the first page.

"What?" I hear you say. "I can message the author of this book I am currently reading, and he will read it. Wow! very personal and interactive."

I know right and if you want him to sign a copy for you, a workmate or even your sweet old Grandmother. Just order another copy and let him know. Anyway better get back to the story.

Like I said I am going to make the next part of the book a bit different. You can choose where the story goes from here. All you have to do is put your hand up now if you want me to go on a Thailand adventure with Thailand Tim. Okay cool, I saw your hand move a little, so that counts. Okay, one more. If you want me to find true love before the book ends put your hand up now. Oh, that's nice of you. Thanks. I no longer believe all of those bad things your workmates say behind your back. Haha.

So I sat there listening to Deb bang on about her daughter's menstrual cycle and then we heard the boarding announcement for our flight.

"That's us Deb," I said standing up, and we made our way onto the plane.

I made my way down the aisle and found my seat. I always try to get a window seat. Why is that?

because the aisle seat sucks. You are just about to fall asleep, and the drinks trolley is bound to come down the aisle and more than likely you are leaning just that little bit too far to your right and bang the drink trolley smashes into your arm waking you straight back up again. I reckon the flight attendants aim for you on purpose. Score, I thought to myself as I see there is no one in the seat next to me as yet. I sit down and buckle myself in and claim both armrests straight away. Armrests are gold when it comes to your comfort during a flight. The trick is to pretend you are asleep when you hear another person trying to sit down next to you. If you be polite and make way for them to settle themselves down, it can backfire on you, and they can steal the armrest between the two of you. Trust me you want both armrests.

So I close my eyes and do fall asleep. Suddenly I wake up to someone trying to elbow my arm off the armrest.

I opened my eyes and I saw an attractive girl about my age, trying to lever my arm off the armrest with her elbow forcefully.

"Do you mind? I was sleeping." I said.

"Well move your arm, and you can go back to sleep," she replied.

"And why exactly would I do that? My arm was here first."

"Because it is my armrest."

"Your armrest? I don't think so."

"Umm, yeah, everyone knows aisle seat gets two armrests, and window seat gets one armrest and the window."

"No one knows that. You just made that up."

"Everyone knows that. You have not been doing

FIFO for long have you? Is this your first time?"

"No. I have been doing this for over four years now. And no one has ever told me that rule. It has always been first in best dressed."

"Well I have been doing FIFO for over six years, and that has always been the rule. So move it."

"Nope you can elbow me as much as you want, but there is no way you can make me move my arm."

"Want to bet? You do realise that I am a girl and all I have to do is tell the flight attendant you are trying to grope me and you will be thrown off the flight."

"As if you would do that," and with that, she reached up and pressed the little light above us that gets the flight attendant's attention. I watched as the attendant made her way towards us.

"Stuff it. You can have it," I said as I pulled my arm off the armrest.

"Is there a problem?" the attendant asked.

"Hi, how does this seat belt work?"

"You clip the two ends together. Here I will show you," the attendant leaned down and did up the girl's seat belt for her. "Is there anything else?"

"No thank you. Thanks for that."

"You're welcome," she said while rolling her eyes and turning to walk back down the aisle.

The girl put her arms down on her two armrests and sat up very straight as if she was a queen sitting on her throne.

"Haha. Very well played," I laughed and leaned over to try and get comfortable on my single armrest.

We arrived at Port Hedland airport, and everyone went to the baggage area to collect their bags.

"Hey Mick," came a voice from behind me. I turned around to see Thailand Tim.

"G'day Tim. How was your break?" I quickly asked before he could ask me.

"Yeah not bad. I watched some movies, went wakeboarding with some mates. I got pretty pissed. Yeah pretty standard. Next break will be even better. I'm going to Thailand. Too bad you're married, or you could come over with me."

"Yeah, too bad."

"She looks alright. What do you reckon?"

I looked over to see who he was talking about and saw the armrest stealer.

"Oh her. Yeah, she's not bad. She was sitting next

to me on the plane. She stole my armrest."

"Yeah, I like brunettes."

"Brunettes? Isn't that brown hair? She's got blonde hair."

"Who are you talking about? I'm talking about the tall chick with the brown hair."

I took another look and saw a tall chick with brown hair standing next to the armrest stealer. This chick must be about six foot tall which is taller than me. I am only five foot ten which I think is a good height. I do not fancy girls that are taller than I am. Bec is five foot nine, and it used to annoy me when she would wear heels and be taller than me. She would pat me on the head and say hello down there. Tim didn't have to worry about that. He would be about six foot three I would guess.

"A bit too tall for me. All yours."

We eventually got our bags and headed to the bus. As we boarded, I saw the armrest stealer and the tall chick sitting together.

"Oh, not you again," she said smiling and looking up at me.

"Well, it looks like we'll be working together."

"Yeah, lucky me," she said while rolling her eyes.

"Wow. What a smart ass," I thought.

We arrive at camp and get ready for work as usual and then jump back on the bus in our work uniforms to head to the mine site.

I make myself a coffee and walk into our pre-start meeting. My supervisor, Danny is already up the front doing his usual speech.

"Welcome back everyone. I hope you had a great break. We will be digging here. Blah, blah, blah and dumping there blah, blah, blah. Also, we have two new starters, Sofia, who will be on the trucks and Jackie who will be on a wheel loader. Make them feel welcome, any questions? No. Great, get to work."

I looked at Jackie and thought there is something not quite right with her. I don't know what it is. Oh well, it will come to me. In the meantime, I am off to drive a truck.

The week was pretty standard. I tried to keep a low profile, so I did not have to talk about the whole Bec thing.

"Hey Mickey Mouse, are you coming to the wet mess tonight, for a couple?" Sofia asked.

"Yep I'll be there."

"You got to go and call the old ball and chain first?"

"Yep."

"Alright, see you down there."

I hadn't told her or anyone that I no longer had a ball and chain to call. Bec did send me a message during the week. It was in regards to signing some divorce paperwork. God, she was not wasting any time. I have concluded that she has no interest in saving this marriage and that she must have been planning this for ages. My interruption with her threesome just quickened the whole thing.

I must admit I think I am handling it all pretty well, seeing this new side of Bec and her coldness towards me has made me feel very differently towards her. There is numbness when I think of her now. No love, no nothing. Just a bit of annoyance that she has wasted so much of my life that I could have spent with someone who does care for me. But even with that, I guess you can't appreciate the sweet without the sour. I saw that on a Tom Cruise movie, Vanilla Sky I think it is called, it has Cameron Diaz in it as well. It's a pretty good saying now I think of it.

Anyway, enough about Bec, I am pretty sure she is not spending her time thinking about me. So I get changed and head down to the wet mess.

This shift change was the same as all the rest. I make my way around to the different tables, drinking beers with the people from various departments. Most people sit down with the people in their department and don't move from their one spot unless they need a piss or another drink. But since I have been on this one site for over four years, I have friends in all of the departments, the crusher, drill and blast, catering, workshop and of course load and haul which I am in.

I was having a good old time, and I noticed Sofia keeps looking over at me to see what I am up to. I put it down to the fact that she is new and doesn't know many other people here yet. I eventually go up to her and see if she wants a game of pool.

"Hey Armrest Stealer. Do you want a game of pool?"

"Yeah why not. We can play doubles," she said while turning to look at Jackie and Tim, who had been all over each other the whole night. "Hey Jackie, do you two want to play doubles?"

"Sounds good. Come on Tim, you can be my partner," Jackie replied.

"Sounds good to me," Tim replied.

I still had a feeling something was up with Jackie. Anyway, we played a couple of games and Jackie was wiping the floor with us. The bell rang for last drinks.

"Hey, I have a bottle of tequila in my room. Let's head there and keep this party going," Tim suggested.

"Sounds good," the girls said in agreement.

"Hey Mick. Do us a favour and sweet talk one of your catering buddies into giving us some lemons and a salt shaker," Tim said.

"Yeah alright. I will ask. I will meet you in your room," I said to Tim.

The three of them headed off to Tim's room, and I wandered over to find Gale, who I know has the keys to the dry mess.

"Hey Gale, buddy, old pal, any chance of letting me into the mess to get some lemons and a salt shaker?"

"There is no way in hell I am going to let your drunk ass in my mess. But come with me, and you can wait outside while I go in and get them for you."

"Sounds good to me. You're a legend Gale."

Gale and I went to the dry mess, and I did stay outside while she popped in and got me a salt shaker and four lemons.

"Thanks for that Gale."

"No worries. Have fun."

Off I went to Tim's room. I could hear his room before I could see it. He had Metallica cranking.

"Oi Tim, you better turn that down."

"What did you say? I can't hear you over the music."

"I said you better turn it down before we get in trouble."

"Yeah alright, alright. I will turn it down. You get the lemon and salt."

"Yep."

"Sweet," with that he went into his room and turned down the music. When he came back out, he was carrying the Tequila and two coffee cups which he had stolen from the dry mess.

"So where are the lemon slices?"

"Lemon slices? You asked for lemons."

"No I did not. I asked for a salt shaker and lemon slices."

"Whatever. Anyway, have you got a knife or something?"

"No. I have a pen. We could cut up the lemons up using a pen or what about a toothbrush. That would work."

"Oh my god. You two are idiots. We can peel the lemons. They are already in individual pieces under the peel," Sofia said shaking her head.

"Oh yeah. I knew that. I was joking about the pen and toothbrush," Tim said as we all laughed.

So we all peeled a lemon each and pulled them apart into individual pieces. We placed them into Tim's work lunch box as he poured shots of Tequila into the coffee cups. I looked at the stained cups trying to figure out if they were clean or not.

"Don't worry. I rinsed the cups out in the shower," Tim said after he saw me looking.

"The shower? Why would you rinse them in the shower and not in the sink?"

"The shower does a better job."

"Umm, okay. Fair enough I guess," I could not be bothered having a drunken conversation about the best way to clean a coffee cup. I was just happy he had washed them.

We all took turns of taking a shot of tequila from one of the coffee cups, licking the salt off the back of our hands and then sucking on a piece of lemon. I could not remember how many I had done, but I was smashed.

"Hey, hey. I have a funny story for you," I said

"Go on," they all said.

And I told them the whole story about Bec cheating on me with Dwayne and his mate.

"Oh, I'm so sorry," both girls were saying.

"I know how to make you feel better Micky boy. Come to Thailand with me this break."

"Haha. Good one. I can't do that."

"Why not?"

Why not? Indeed. I had absolutely no reason why I couldn't.

"Yeah okay. Why not?"

"Awesome I will get my flight itinerary, and you pull out your phone and credit card."

"What, you want me to book it right now?"

"Yep, otherwise you will chicken out."

So I booked my plane ticket to Thailand.

"Let's celebrate Mick's new life," Tim said. The girls cheered and we did another round.

But, I guess that last shot was my one too many and I stood up, took two steps forward, and power spewed all over the red dirt in front of Tim's room.

"I think I will call it a night," I said.

"Me too," said Sofia, "are you coming Jackie?"

"Na. I think I will stay and have a couple of more with Tim."

"Haha. Okay have fun," Sofia smiled at Jackie.

With that, Sofia and I stumbled off to our own rooms and left Tim and Jackie to have a couple more. If you know what I mean. Wink, wink. If you do not know what I mean. They are going to have sex.

I woke up the next day feeling like death warmed up. Why is it so bright in here I thought to myself. I looked up and realised that I had left the door wide open and that the sun was beaming straight into my room. I could hear the sound of flies buzzing. I looked at the floor, and there was spew everywhere and right in the middle of it was my bathroom floor mat. I guess in my drunken state last night I must have tried to clean up the spew using the floor mat, then given up and passed out.

The whole room stunk of spew. Which was making me want to throw up again? I quickly jumped out of bed. I had planned to make it to the toilet or shower to throw up. However, I only made it a meter. I slipped over on spew that was on the floor.

I cover my mouth so as not to throw up on myself. But the pressure was too much to contain the new spew in my mouth, and the spew came out through my nose and then out of my mouth anyway. My ears felt a bit different. God, I hope I didn't burst an eardrum by trying to contain all of that spew pressure in my mouth.

I pulled myself back up to my feet using the bathroom door frame. I looked down at the mess and thought stuff this I'm going to have a wet dog. So I opened the fridge and grabbed a beer and slowly made my way into the shower. I didn't want to slip over again.

I adjusted the shower temperature so it was as cold as I could handle. When I was happy with the temperature, I sat down on the floor of the shower and drunk my beer with the shower washing over me like a waterfall.

I must have stayed in there for about half an hour. I even think I nodded off a couple of times. Honestly, I didn't want to get out and deal with the mess. Plus it felt as if my head would explode if I stopped having the cold water flowing over it.

I did eventually get out and get dressed. I put on the darkest sunglasses I could find and popped my head out the door. Luck was on my side. I saw Crystal, one of the cleaners with her trolley.

"Hey Crystal, come here, please."

"Hey Mick, what's up?"

"Hey can I borrow your mop and bucket."

"Yeah no worries. Oh my god, your room stinks."

"Yeah I know. That is why I need the mop."

She gave me the mop and bucket, and I cleaned up my room. I left the door open to air it out, and that bathroom floor mat went straight in the bin. The room smelled like lemon disinfectant scented spew.

When I was happy enough with the room, I popped a couple of Panadol, skulled lots of water and one more beer. Then I went straight back to bed and stayed there until my alarm went off, telling me to get up and get ready for work. I didn't want to go to work I just wanted to stay in my bed forever or at least all night.

I walked into the dry mess and ordered two steaks. While they were getting cooked I packed my lunch and filled up my travel coffee cup. I think I will need a few coffees tonight to stay awake.

I went back and collected my steaks and added some vegetables to my plate. I walked over to our usual table, and Tim was already there eating his dinner.

"Hey Tim, I thought you would be sitting with Jackie."

"Piss off," Tim replied angrily.

"Woo, woo. Did I miss something here? You two looked cozy last night. What happened?"

"Sorry Mick. I don't want to talk about it."

"Wow. Must be serious I have never heard you talk like that before."

"Yeah sorry. Now can we change the subject?"

"Umm. Okay then."

We sat in awkward silence for a bit. I figured I might as well start eating my steaks.

"So are you excited about the trip?"

"Trip? What trip?"

"Haha. What trip? our Thailand trip, this break."

"What do you mean? I'm not going to Thailand."

"Yes you are. You booked your ticket last night."

"Umm, I think I would remember booking a plane ticket."

"Check your emails on your phone. You should have received your confirmation and flight itinerary."

I pulled out my phone, and sure enough, there was an email from Virgin confirming my flight to Thailand.

"Wow. I guess I am going to Thailand."

"Yep. It's going to be awesome. We can go and watch the Muay Thai, hire some motorbikes, go parasailing, get massages and you can even get a bar girl if you want."

It did all sound pretty awesome. Except for the bar girl, do not worry I am not turning gay or anything. I am just not interested in Asians and not one that has been with a thousand different guys.

"Yeah sounds pretty cool. What about accommodation?"

"Don't worry about that. I upgraded my room last night to a suite with two double beds."

"Awesome. Boys trip," we high fived each other and laughed. Then we finished dinner and went to the self-testing machine.

"0.02," Said Tim.

"0.01," I replied.

"Sweet. We will both be blowing zeros by the time we make it work."

With peace of mind that we wouldn't be blowing numbers, we hopped onto the bus to go to work. I saw the girls sitting in their usual seat.

"Hi ladies," I said.

"Hi Mick," they both replied.

Tim just walked past ignoring both of them.

"Hi Tim," Sofia said.

"Oh. Hi Sofia," Tim replied. Tim and Jackie didn't say anything to each other. That awkward feeling suddenly came back, this time it was hanging over all four of us.

The shift was pretty standard. Drive the truck here and there. All the time I am trying to stay awake. I had three coffees and two cans of red bull. That last hour was a killer I could hardly stay awake. I cranked up the heavy metal and sang and danced around in my truck while I was driving. If someone filmed truckies on night shift, they would think these people are crazy or just idiots.

The rest of the week went pretty much the same. Tim and Jackie avoided each other, and all of us just tried to stay awake while operating our machines.

I was starting to get excited about going to Thailand with Tim. Like I had said before I had only been overseas once, and that was a family trip to Bali.

The day finally arrives for Tim's and my great adventure. I won't bore you with the airport and customs stuff. It's the same as the FIFO plane trips, just a more extended trip.

We arrive in Thailand and collect our bags. Then I see a man holding a sign with our names on it.

"Look Tim, that's our names."

"Yeah cool, that's our lift then."

"Hi. That's us," I say to the man while pointing at the sign.

"Welcome to Thailand. Please follow me," says the sign man and he lead us to a minivan parked out the front. We put our bags in the back and hop in.

"First time in Thailand?"

"For me it is, but Tim here has been heaps," I answered.

"That is good. Do you want to do a tour? You can book with me now. Easy," he says while passing me a hand full of different flyers, each advertising the various activities and tours available. There were themed dinner and shows, water sports, dirt bike riding, shooting a gun and the list goes on.

"Wow. Hey Tim. What do you want to do first?" I must have sounded a little too excited because Tim started laughing his ass off.

"Haha. Calm down there tiger. We will get settled into the hotel first. Then we can pick a couple of activities to do. Remember we have five days here and if you like it and don't annoy me too much. I might even bring you back another time," he said this to me as if I was an excited little child.

"Haha. Okay, smart ass," I laughed back.

When we arrived at the hotel, it looked like a palace. All of the workers kept bowing their heads at us saying "Sawadee ka," Tim told me it just meant, hello. It is beautiful here. The complete opposite to the red dirt and the dongas we have at work.

The room Tim had organised was massive, and it overlooked a swimming pool. Tim saw me staring at the pool.

"There are five more pools here Mick and all of them have a swim up bar. You keen for a drink and a swim?"

"Hell yeah. Let's go."

We put on our board shorts and head down to one of the pools. This pool overlooked the beach. We grabbed a beer each and relaxed submerged in the pool watching the other tourist's jet skiing and parasailing in the ocean.

"Ahh. This is the life, hey Tim."

"Yep. It sure is."

We relaxed in the pool, drinking the local beer for about an hour. Then a bell sounded, ding ding.

"Happy hour. Half priced shots," called out the bartender.

"You keen," Tim asked me.

"Bring it on."

Tim and I went shot for shot for the full happy hour, never leaving the pool to urinate. I looked around at the other tourists in the pool, and I cannot remember seeing any of them leave the pool to go to the toilet.

So basically, we are swimming around in a big pool of chlorinated urine. The best thing was I am too pissed to care. Get it, too pissed, to care about the piss. Okay, not that funny.

When you think of the ocean with all of the fish and other sea life, they do not get out of the ocean to pee and poo, I guess the ocean is just one massive toilet. Wow! The intelligent thoughts you have when you are drunk.

"Come on Mick. Let's get ready and I will show you the nightlife."

"Bring it on," I replied. Gee, I say "Bring it on," a lot.

We hopped out of the pool and grabbed our towels. We were only halfway back to our room. When suddenly I felt sick and threw up in the manicured, bushes next to the walkway.

"Yuk. Dad, look at what that man is doing," a little girl said. I looked up to see a family walking towards us.

"Piss off," I felt like saying, but I bit my tongue. You do not want to be that guy. You know the one that throws up in the bushes and yells at little girls. That guy is a dick. I finished up my spew and carried on walking or stumbling the rest of the way to the room.

"Here, drink some water," Tim said while handing me a big bottle of water I skulled the majority of it and headed straight for the shower. I did not want to ruin Tim's night because I could not handle my alcohol.

We had a nice Thailand themed dinner which involved five traditionally dressed dancers doing their traditional dance. The food was lovely if not a little bit too spicy.

"Feeling better Spewy?" Tim asked.

"Yep I think the trick is to eat when you are drinking. The liquid only diet does not seem to work for me. Haha," we both laughed.

"You up for some Muay Thai?" Tim asked.

"Oh yeah I like kickboxing."

"Well, technically Muay Thai is not kickboxing. Kickboxing is kicks and punches. While Muay Thai has knees and elbows as well."

"Oh, okay. I stand corrected. Yep, sounds good."

"Cool. We will finish these beers and head over."

It was only a ten-minute walk down the road to the Muay Thai ring. It took us thirty minutes because I kept stopping to look at the stalls selling the fake Hugo Boss belts, Rolex watches, and Billabong t-shirts. Tim helped me to barter down the guy selling the Rolexes. I ended up getting a really flash one for fifty dollars. The guy initially asked me for two hundred dollars. Which I thought was fair since a real one would be worth ten to twenty thousand dollars. Tim would not let me buy it at that price.

"No way will I let you buy that watch for that price," Tim said, "let me handle this."

"He will give you a thousand baht."

"Haha. I would buy it off you for a thousand baht," the stall guy replied, "make it two thousand, you are an Australian. You have lots of money."

Tim and I started to walk off.

"Okay, okay. Fifteen hundred baht, no less," the stall guy said angrily.

"That is fair. Pay the guy Mick."

Just like that, I was pimping with a flash looking watch hanging from my wrist.

"Now can we go to the Muay Thai ring?" Tim asked. "I promise you will have plenty of time to buy all of you fake stuff before we fly home."

"Yeah alright. Thanks for getting me the watch so cheap. The next round is on me," I replied. I could not stop looking at the watch, it looked like something Brad Pitt or some other rich guy would wear.

We finally made it to the muay thai ring. Bang, bang, thud, thud. Wow! These guys are really going hard. We found a seat on the benches surrounding the ring and true to my word I ordered us a round of beers.

After each fight, the fighters walk around the crowd, and we give them a hundred baht each for watching their match.

The announcer came out into the ring.

"Hello everyone, we need a volunteer from the crowd to fight one of our fighters," the announcer called out to the crowd. What kind of idiot would put their hand up to do that?

"Hey, over here," Tim yelled out.

What? Tim wants to do it. What an idiot.

"Wonderful. We have a volunteer. Please come down."

"Well get up and go down," Tim said to me.

"What? You are the idiot that put your hand up."

"Yeah, that was for you. Don't worry; they go really soft on the tourists. Think about it, they would not make any money off the tourists if they beat them up. Now would they?"

"That makes sense. I guess," I stood up, skulled the rest of my beer and made my way down into the ring. The audience gave me a big cheer. I turned around and did a fist pump in the air to the crowd. Haha, that reminded me of what I did before the sheep almost knocked me out. I guess some things never change.

The announcer put some gloves on me and said, "In you go."

Wow! The safety department would have a field day or a heart attack with this. That is in regards to the lack of personal protective equipment and training. The guy I am versing is a lot shorter than I am and looked about 12 years old, he would be about 19 years old. You know these Asians always look younger than what they are. I think I will go soft on him; I don't want to hurt the poor fella.

The announcer dinged the bell.

"Fight," he called out.

Pow, bang, bang, thud and I was on my arse. He had push kicked me in the stomach and then punched me twice in my side. I was literally seeing stars and thought I might throw up.

I got back up, and the crowd cheered for him or me. I do not know who. Then pow, bang, bang, thud. I was back on my arse again. He had push kicked me in the stomach again with his right foot, kicked me on my side with his left leg and finished me with a kick to my head with his right leg.

I came to, a minute or two later with the announcer using some tiger balm, smelling stuff under my nose.

"He is all good," he announced to the crowd. They cheered, and Tim helped me back to my seat on the bench.

"That was awesome. I cannot believe you had the balls to go in there. I would never have done that," Tim said while handing me a beer.

"What? And I thought you said they go soft on tourists?"

"Oh, yeah, I lied, they go harder. Haha," Tim laughed, "at least you have a good story to tell Sofia."

"Why would she care?" I asked

"Umm. Maybe because she fancies you."

"No way. She is totally out of my league."

"Yeah, I think so too. Jackie told me she does though."

"Speaking of Jackie. What happened between you two?"

"Don't go there Mick. It will just ruin the good time we are having."

"Okay. I'll drop it."

Tim and I thought we might as well call it a night and he helped me into a tuk-tuk which is a three-wheel motorbike, taxi. And we headed back to our hotel.

I woke up the next morning, and I could hardly move. I looked down and saw a massive purple bruise on my side, and I had a shocking headache. I heard Tim coming out of the shower.

"How are you feeling?" Tim asked.

"Like crap. I have the sorest head and check out the bruise," I said while lifting my shirt up.

"Well lucky you are in Thailand. You can get almost anything from the chemists here. After breakfast, I will pop down and get you some pain killers."

We go down to the breakfast area, which is overlooking another one of the hotel's swimming pools. There is everything available for breakfast; six different types of freshly squeezed juices, ten kinds of cereal, bacon and eggs, omelettes and the list goes on. This buffet puts the mine site's buffet to shame.

I grabbed a big plate of bacon and eggs and two glasses of pineapple juice. And sat down at a table so close to the pool, I could bend down and touch the water.

"Ahh, besides the bruised side and throbbing headache, this is paradise. Haha."

"Haha. Yep, it sure is."

"I can see why you keep coming back."

Tim just smiled in reply.

"I am going to pop down to the chemist now. How strong do you want your painkillers? Slight pain relief or cannot feel your face pain relief?" Tim asked.

"Just normal thanks. I still want to have some fun today and not be totally out of it."

"Yep. No worries. See you soon," with that Tim was off.

I finished my breakfast and jumped straight into the pool and ordered a beer from the swim up bar. Tim came back about twenty minutes later.

"Here you go," Tim said while handing me the pills. "I am going to grab a towel."

As he walked off, I pulled the pills out of the envelope. They are about the same shape and size as a Panadol. I guess two would do the trick, I thought and popped them into my mouth. Tim came back with his towel.

"Just take half a pill to start off with, and in four hours you can have another half." he said.

"What? I just took two."

"Why would you take something, when you don't know what it is?"

"Because you gave it to me."

"Wow! If I jumped off a cliff, would you do it?"

"No. Oh no. What do you think will happen now?"

"Calm down drama queen. I reckon you will feel really relaxed."

He was right. I did become really relaxed. It felt as if I was melting into my sunbed and I must have fallen asleep because I started to have the craziest dream. I was Mickey Mouse, and Sofia was Minnie Mouse. Tim was Goofy, and Jackie was a female Goofy. Bec came into the dream, and she was Daisy

Duck, who was a villain in the dream. Then I woke up. Wow! I wonder if this is what LSD is like.

I felt cold water being poured over my face.

"Earth to Mick, are you in there?" Tim said.

"What do you think you are doing? First, you drug me, now you are pouring water over me."

"Oh boohoo. First off, you drugged yourself, and second, I am stopping you from becoming dehydrated. Third, you have been lying there all day, and the staff are starting to give you funny looks, especially when you were calling out for Minnie Mouse."

He put a pizza down beside me.

"Here eat this."

I ate pizza and skulled some water. I could now feel the fog from the pills lifting. It was actually nice to feel some pain. After the pizza, I went up to the room and had a nap. At least I will not get sunburnt in the room.

"Get up," Tim said, shaking me. "It's seven o'clock. You have slept the whole day. Let's go have some fun."

"Sounds good."

I had a quick shower and got changed. Then we headed out to one of the many bars that line the streets.

"Hey, does she look familiar?" Tim asked me.

I looked over and saw it was Joy. The bar girl Bob was in love with, and she was arm in arm with some other short fat guy in his mid-fifties.

"Well, at least she has a type. He could be Bob's twin," I say.

"Yep and any bet that sucker is sending her money over each month as well," Tim said while taking a photo of Joy and Bob's twin on his phone. "Might as well break his heart sooner rather than later and it will save him money in the long run."

We go from one bar to the next, using up their happy hour deals. Suddenly a local guy jumps out of nowhere.

"You want to see ping pong show?" He asks.

"No thanks," I answered

"Yes. He does. Let's go," Tim said to the guy, and off we go following this random guy through the laneways. Truthfully, I had no interest in seeing a ping-pong ball pop out of a girl's vagina. I guess that is why I am boring according to Bec.

We enter an arena similar to the Muay Thai one. On the stage are the ladies doing their thing. I had expected to see the room full of seedy men. To my surprise, there was a real mixture. A married couple, a group of girls that looked like they were on a hen's night, some Japanese tourists and us. The hen's night girls were having a great time, and one caught the ping-pong ball.

Next, a lady from the stage brought out a balloon and handed it to the married couple, who were told to hold it up high above their heads. The girl on the stage propped up her legs and shot out a little dart, popping the balloon.

"Wow! She has a good aim," I said.

"Yeah. I am sure she has had plenty of practice."

We stayed there for another twenty minutes then decided to hit a couple more bars.

"Pretty talented girls," I said.

"Yeah. They are."

"The people watching are not as seedy as I thought they would be."

"Yeah. I guess everyone hears about these shows and wants to know for themselves what all the fuss is about."

"Yeah. Sounds about right."

We start doing lots of shots at the next bar, and I was getting hammered. The last thing I remember was playing pool with some of the local girls. They were taller and better at pool at this bar than the other local girls at previous bars.

I woke up feeling like crap. I could smell spew everywhere. I looked around, but could not see any. Then I looked down at my t-shirt, and it was covered in spew. The smell was so bad that I quickly pulled off the t-shirt while at the same time wiping the spew across my face. Which made me gag and I was about to throw up again.

"Hell yeah, bring it on."

"If it is okay with you I might just give the bars a miss for the rest of the trip. We can do some tours, and you can shop until you drop if you want? Haha."

"Haha. Sounds good to me."

The rest of the trip was great. We hired jet skis, did a boat tour to some islands, white water rafting and I bought heaps of fake brand label clothes. I even bought Sofia a fake Chanel handbag. The best bit was no more hangovers.

We were on the plane back to Perth, and I turned to Tim.

"Hey, did you have sex with that Thai chick?"

"Yeah, of course, I did. But do not tell Jackie. I think I am going to apologise to her and see what happens there. Why are you asking me that?"

"No reason. I was just wondering."

"Oh, okay."

We sat back, put our headphones on and watched our movies.

I sat there just thinking. Boom!! My mind was officially blown. Suddenly the feeling I had that something was not quite right with Jackie and the crazy dream I had when I was high on pain killers, all made sense. Sofia and I are meant to be together, just like Mickey and Minnie Mouse. Tim and Jackie are meant to be together. The fact that Tim was Goofy meant he was a tall bloke. The fact that Jackie was a girl goofy meant she was a tall, lady bloke or ladyboy. Like the ladyboy, Tim had sex with. Jackie is Transgender or whatever they are called. Wow! What a spin out.

Hey reader did you see that coming? Cool hey? Well I will tell you how it all ends up. That way you are not thinking, so what happened next?

Here it goes. I ended up with Sofia, and we hope to live happily ever after. Once the divorce goes through, I never want to see Bec again. I heard she joined some hippy cult or something?

Tim showed Bob the photo of Joy and Bob's twin. He got rid of Joy and is now with another Thailand girl so far so good with this one.

Tim and Jackie are engaged. They are planning to get married next year, why not it is legal in Australia now.

And there you have it. I hope you enjoyed the book. Let me know what you thought on my social media and tell all of your friends to buy a copy. Cheers.

About the Author

Aaron started his mining career as a driller's offsider, on an RC drill rig. Then he landed a job doing FIFO, as a blast crew labourer and earnt his shot firers licence. When he realised a dump truck operator got paid the same as a shot firer, he made the transition into the air conditioning and has been operating the big mining machines ever since.

He is currently writing a series of novels about the different careers people have and all of the crazy and funny things that happen within those careers. From police officers to paramedics and many more. Keep an eye out for these fantastic novels.

I quickly ran into the bathroom and threw up in the sink. I lifted my head and saw a girl, who was wearing a t-shirt and knickers peeing in the toilet. The only thing was that she was not sitting down to pee. She was standing. She shook whatever was in front of her that she was peeing out of and tucked it back into her knickers and turned around.

"Hello Spew Boy," she said. Then she walked past me, I watched to see which bed she would hop into, praying to God that it was not mine.

She pulled back the covers to Tim's bed and put her arm around him spooning him. Wow! I quickly had a shower to wash the spew off me. Then chucked on some clothes and snuck out the door, trying not to wake Tim.

I got some breakfast and sat by the pool. Wow! What a crazy night. I think I will hang down here for a while. I do not want to be in that room when Tim wakes up and realises the girl in his bed is not a girl.

I ordered a beer and chilled out in the pool. An hour later Tim comes over and jumps in the pool.

"Hey Mick, what a night?" he said and ordered himself a beer and a burger.

"Yeah, where is the girl?" I asked.

"Oh her she is gone. I cannot wait for this burger I am starving."

Wow! He was pretty relaxed about the whole thing. Maybe he could not remember what he did last night, and she just left without him seeing what she had downstairs.

"You want to go jet-skiing and parasailing today," he asked.